STO

FRIENDS
OF ACPL

W9-AGW-500

3 1833 00693 5107

*jimmy fox
and the
mountain rescue*

jimmy fox
and the
mountain rescue

By Don Dwiggins

illustrated by Olga Dwiggins

A Golden Gate Junior Book
Childrens Press, Chicago

Library of Congress Cataloging in Publication Data

Dwiggins, Don.
  Jimmy Fox and the mountain rescue.

  "A Golden Gate junior book."
  SUMMARY: While attempting to rescue two people downed
in a small plane, 15-year-old Jimmy and a fellow volun-
teer violate Civil Air Patrol rules and parachute into
a mountain valley during a snowstorm.
  [1. Rescue work—Fiction. 2. Parachuting—
Fiction] I. Dwiggins, Olga. II. Title.
PZ7.D9597J   [Fic]   78-11155
ISBN 0-516-08831-9

Copyright © 1979 by Regensteiner Publishing Enterprises, Inc.
All rights reserved
Published simultaneously in Canada
Printed in the United States of America
Designed by Jon Ritchie

CO. SCHOOLS
C872342

to Marjorie Thayer

contents

jimmy fox
and the
mountain rescue

fear
of
falling

Jimmy Fox stared through the plane's window at the awesome scene spread out below. To most people the snow-capped peaks of the mighty Sierra Nevada mountains were beautiful. But, to Jimmy, danger lurked there. He held his breath and shut his eyes. If anything happened, there was no place to land. He gripped the control wheel of the Cessna 180 so hard his knuckles turned white. He listened carefully to the sound of the engine. Suddenly the plane lurched sideways, as if shoved by a giant hand. Then it plunged downward–toward the rocky peaks, almost out of control.

Jimmy dared not look. He was certain they were going to crash. Beside him Jimmy's father, Frank Fox, expertly righted the plunging plane. In a moment they flew out of the dangerous downdraft.

"Air's pretty rough, Jimmy," Frank Fox said quietly. Jimmy nodded. But he couldn't answer. He bit his lip. He didn't want his father to know he was afraid. It was a crazy fear, he knew. Crazy for a pilot. He never felt it flying the sailplanes that were almost a part of the sky. But the fear had been growing inside him. Ever since he started learning to fly powered airplanes.

Powered airplanes didn't just rise and fall gently with the air currents. They plunged right through them. It was like driving a fast car on a bumpy road. The planes bounced up and down, flying through updrafts and downdrafts. It made him feel sick inside.

At fifteen Jimmy was still too young to fly a powered airplane solo. But he could fly the right-hand seat as a Civil Air Patrol Observer, on search missions. This was his third search mission, hunting for a lost plane.

"Turn up the radio, Jimmy," his father

said. "See if you can pick up an emergency signal on 121.5."

Jimmy opened his eyes slowly. His fear of falling was gradually going away as the plane circled around to the upwind side of a mountain peak where the air was smoother. He reached out and turned up the volume control on the radio. All he could hear was a loud crash of static. It came from an electrical storm raging over the mountains close by. Jimmy switched the radio off. It was next to useless now.

In the distance he could see the towering black storm cloud. Lightning bolts stabbed down from it. He felt his stomach tighten. Severe winds would be reaching out toward them. The winds could grab the plane and shake it the way a dog shakes a bone.

Someplace down below, maybe under the storm cloud, lay a shattered airplane. If the pilot were still alive he could soon die from exposure to the freezing cold. They must find him soon.

Jimmy pushed his fears from his mind. He tried again to tune the radio. Flying on CAP missions like this one was always exciting. You had to fly low, close to the ground, down through mountain passes and between towering peaks, searching for an emergency radio signal.

Another pilot already had reported hearing such a signal in this area. That was why Jimmy and his father were here. The signal came from a device on an airplane called an Emergency Locator Transmitter, or ELT for short. If a plane crashed, the ELT went off. It shrieked *WOW! WOW! WOW!*—over and over. But Jimmy knew that ELT's sometimes went off accidentally, flying through rough air.

Search planes sometimes crashed too, Jimmy knew. A wing could break off if the plane flew into a strong enough downdraft. Jimmy's fear of falling returned in a wave as the Cessna 180 slammed through more rough air. He glanced out at the plane's silver wings. They were strong, but mountain turbulence had caused even stronger ships to crash. He'd seen a wrecked plane once. The plane lay on its back, one wing sheared off. It was a sight he'd never forget.

Jimmy's father owned the Cessna 180. It was one of 6,000 planes enrolled in the nationwide CAP program. The CAP was a civilian auxiliary to the United States Air Force. Jimmy felt proud to wear the "fatigue" uniform of a CAP Cadet. Whenever a plane was missing, CAP pilots and observers in the vicinity took to the sky to try and find it. They saved many lives that way.

Jimmy knew a lot about the ways of the sky at first hand. It had been a year since he had won his glider wings, flying his own sailplane, the *Flying Falcon*. And he knew that a downed pilot would be lucky to stay alive in a Sierra storm, if he were injured. It was 40 below zero down there, where the snow storm cut visibility to zero.

Again their plane was hammered by the brutal winds. The force was hard to believe. Jimmy wondered how much more the Cessna 180 could stand. He forced himself to think of other things. He thought about Morning Sun Airfield, down on the Mojave Desert, where he had lived all his young life.

All members of Jimmy's family were expert flyers. They put on regular air shows at Morning Sun. They billed themselves as *The Flying Foxes*. Soon Jimmy would be old enough to join them. Air show flying was different from flying search missions in dangerous mountain country. Every stunt was carefully planned.

Jimmy was never afraid when he flew loops and rolls and spins with his father. He knew exactly what to expect. It was the unexpected that really scared him. Especially flying through wild mountain turbulence. And he knew he must get over his secret fear of falling or he would never be a good air show pilot.

16

Jimmy's sister Frances was two years older than he was. Already she was an expert aerobatic flyer. His mother, Debbie Fox, was a well-known wing rider and parachutist. Frank Fox was leader of *The Flying Foxes* air show troupe. Frank was a veteran pilot. He'd taught Army Air Corps cadets how to fly during the Second World War, in the 1940's. He had bought Morning Sun Airfield right after the war ended. He had settled his family there.

Jimmy thought about Bud Horner, his best friend at Morning Sun. Bud was chief pilot and mechanic. Both Bud and Jimmy's father gave him regular flying lessons in powered planes. In another year he could qualify for his private pilot license.

Jimmy's father often let him take over the controls on search missions like this one. Now, when his father reached for his binoculars to search the ground below for the missing plane, Jimmy gripped the control wheel with tense fingers. He tried to hold the plane smoothly on course, against the thrashing winds. It was late afternoon. The winds were getting stronger, whipping snow from mountain peaks in blinding white curtains.

It was almost impossible to see the granite mountaintops through the blowing snow. It seemed almost as though the jagged peaks were reaching toward them, through the white mists, to grab their wings and make them crash. Jimmy flew the plane around the side of a huge peak, hoping to get out of the wind. But instead, he flew right into a strong downdraft.

The right wing snapped down at a steep angle. Jimmy fought hard against the force that wanted to rip the wheel from his hands. The plane kept plunging down–down, down, toward a rocky outcropping.

"Dad," Jimmy cried. "We're going to crash!"

His father took over the controls and wrestled the plane away from the peak–just in time. He swung the plane away from the

storm-lashed mountaintops, out over the broad valley to the east.

"That was a bad one, Jimmy," his father said, smiling grimly. "We were right inside the Sierra Wave!"

Oh, no! Jimmy thought. Not the Sierra Wave! He had heard many wild stories about that giant, unseen air current. It was a fierce wave of high winds that curved up and over the mountain range, then plunged headlong down into the valley. It was an invisible waterfall.

High above the plane Jimmy could see a strange-looking cloud. It curved across the sky, shaped like a lens. Because of its shape, Jimmy knew, it was called a lenticular. It was always there when the Sierra Wave was blowing and the winds off the Pacific Ocean were moist. The winds blew more than a hundred miles an hour.

Jimmy looked down below them. He saw another frightening cloud boiling at the base of the mountains. It was almost black, filled

with blowing dust scoured up from the valley floor. It was like the seething foam at the bottom of a huge waterfall. This one was called a roll cloud. It was the most dangerous cloud of them all, an angry, churning vortex of wild winds.

"Let's head for home, Jimmy," his father

said, above the noise of the engine and the slipstream. "It's getting dark. The Sierra Wave is too strong now to fly in!"

Jimmy breathed a sigh of relief. He wiped sweat from his face and tried to smile. "We can search again in the morning, Dad," he said. "Maybe the pilot can find shelter for the night. That is, if he's still alive."

Jimmy had just settled down for the flight home when a giant uprush of air gripped the Cessna 180 and sent it hurtling skyward. They were trapped inside a secondary wave! He knew right away what that meant, from what he had heard about the tricky Sierra Wave. Whenever the winds swept down off the mountains into the valley, they were bound to curve sharply upward again.

Frank Fox reduced power to slow the plane down. The air speed dropped to what Jimmy recognized as its maneuvering speed. His father pointed the nose down, but still they were lifted higher and higher. The altimeter hands seemed to spin around and

around. They were being forced upward...
ten thousand...eleven thousand...twelve
thousand...thirteen thousand feet!

The air grew icy cold. Jimmy shivered as
they rose through misty ice clouds. The
plane's windshield was coated over with
frost. They could not see out. They were
inside an icy white cocoon.

Frank Fox finally shoved the throttle forward all the way. "We'll have to power-dive
out, Jimmy!" he yelled. The engine strained.
Slowly they began to dive away from the
central core of the secondary wave. Jimmy
felt limp. At last they settled down into
smooth, level flight at the far side of the
valley. It was growing dark. In the distance
they could see the lights of Morning Sun
Airfield.

jenny's challenge

Jimmy's father picked up the microphone. He tuned the radio to the CAP home base frequency. It was time to report in, using the special CAP code names assigned to them. The Morning Sun Home Base was *White Bear Ten-Ten*. Their Cessna 180 was *Brown Bear Ten-Eight*.

Frank Fox spoke into the mike. "White Bear Ten-Ten, this is Brown Bear Ten-Eight. Come in, White Bear!"

Frances's voice answered quickly, "Brown Bear Ten-Eight, this is White Bear Ten-Ten. Over."

"We got blown out, Fran," Frank Fox reported. "Big storm blowing! We'll have to scrub the search until tomorrow."

"Roger, Dad," Frances replied. "But there's more trouble! Jenny Gorman made a sport parachute jump today. She landed on top of Wild Horse Mesa and can't get down! She'll freeze up there tonight when the storm hits."

Jimmy glanced at his father. He thought, Jenny Gorman was in trouble–*again!* For the third time in a month. Couldn't she do anything right? She ought to know better! She was the daughter of Wilson Gorman, his father's business partner in their small charter airline.

Jenny Gorman was just Jimmy's age. She was home from school for the Christmas holidays. Jenny was sort of pretty, Jimmy admitted to himself. But he though she was crazy to jump. Secretly he envied her because, obviously, she had no fear of falling. She seemed to love parachuting. Jimmy could not imagine himself jumping out of an airplane and falling down the sky.

"Okay, Fran, we'll fly over and have a look," Frank Fox was saying into the mike. "It's right on our way home."

Jimmy felt anger growing inside him.

Because Jenny Gorman had pulled another dumb stunt, they'd have to risk a dangerous night landing to rescue her. He could picture in his mind what had happened. She'd jumped from her father's twin-engine Cessna Bobcat and the frontal winds from the storm had blown her over onto the mesa.

He peered ahead through the evening sky. He could make out the flat tabletop mountain in the distance. High above it he saw the lights of an airplane circling. That would be Wilson Gorman's Bobcat. Jimmy knew the plane was too big to land and pick up Jenny.

Frank Fox switched radio frequencies and called Gorman. "This is Frank, Wilson," he said. "We're coming right over. The CAP mission is aborted!"

"Please hurry, Frank!" Gorman answered. "It's already pretty dark and I can't land down there."

Jimmy felt sudden anxiety. It would be tricky, even for the Cessna 180, to land on the mountaintop, in a stiff crosswind out of the west. But he knew it had to be done. They couldn't leave Jenny there overnight.

Soon they were circling above the flat top of the mesa. Scattered mesquite bushes made dark clumps of shadow. The ground looked level enough. The plane's right wing dipped low in a sudden turn. Jimmy grabbed his father's arm. "Look—there she is!" he cried.

A white parachute canopy was draped over a big bush. Jenny stood nearby, waving at them. She looked all right. But the dangerous part was ahead—landing to rescue her.

"You take over, Jimmy," Frank Fox said. "This will be good experience for you."

Jimmy found his fears vanishing in the face of this challenge. His father trusted him. He wouldn't let him down. He was good at short-field landings. He'd practiced them every chance he got. He straightened in his seat, adjusted power. He swung the plane around and lined it up for a landing approach. Dead ahead, a dark bare spot looked good.

Carefully Jimmy slowed the plane down,

lowered flaps, then trimmed the 180 for a low, slow pass. He wanted a closer look for hidden danger before actually landing. He could see Jenny's face staring up as they flew past her. Now he opened the throttle and circled for the landing. They were headed straight into the blowing wind. The landing was a beauty! There was barely a jolt as the wheels touched down.

Jimmy braked to a stop. He and his father jumped out. They ran to where Jenny was untangling her parachute riser cords. She took off her crash helmet and shook down her long blonde hair.

"Hi!" she called. "Help me get untangled, will you please? Boy—did that wind ever fool me!"

"So you did it again," Jimmy said. He shook his head. "This makes the third time, Jenny!"

Frank Fox interrupted. "Get the plane ready for takeoff. We don't have much light left. I'll help Jenny with the parachute.

Jimmy went back to the plane and got the engine started. Carefully he taxied into takeoff position, then waited with the engine idling slowly.

He had mixed feelings about Jenny. He was glad she was all right, but he couldn't help feeling resentment toward her. Here she was, only a girl, and an experienced jumper! He felt almost glad that she'd gotten into trouble again. Maybe that would teach her not to be so smart. It made his stomach tighten to imagine falling down the sky—even with a parachute.

He held the door open for Jenny to climb in back. "I'm sorry to cause all this trouble," she said to Frank Fox, fastening her seat belt.

"Sure you're okay?" Frank asked as he slid into the left front seat.

"Just a twisted ankle," Jenny replied. "It's a good thing Dad saw where I landed and let you know!"

Wilson Gorman's Bobcat buzzed low overhead, its wings rocking in a salute.

"Thanks, fellows!" he called over the radio. "See you at Morning Sun!"

Jimmy's take-off, with quarter flaps, was as good as his landing. The plane lifted easily into the cold night sky. Jimmy turned it toward home. He felt proud. He couldn't have done a better job back at Morning Sun, landing on its long, paved runway.

Gorman was waiting for them, his twin-engine Bobcat parked on the flight line. Jimmy pulled up alongside and shut down his engine.

Frank held the door open for Jenny. Suddenly she leaned over and brushed Jimmy's cheek with a soft kiss. "Thanks, Jimmy," she said. "I'd be freezing up there on the mesa if it weren't for you!"

"You better be more careful with that parachute," Jimmy said, his face reddening. "You'll kill yourself yet!"

Jenny was silent for a moment, looking at him. Instinctively she knew that Jimmy must be afraid of parachute jumping.

"A parachute is a life-saver, not a killer,

Jimmy," she said finally. "Why don't you let me check you out in one? I'll show you how to jump safely. Why don't you come over tomorrow morning, when the winds are down?"

Jimmy couldn't answer. He was quaking inside at the thought of making a parachute jump. Jenny's invitation was an outright dare, he knew, and there was no way out. He had to accept the challenge or look like a coward.

"Well, if the storm passes, okay," he said. "Unless the Civil Air Patrol needs me to continue the search."

Jenny laughed. "I'm sure they can spare you, Jimmy. Right, Mr. Fox?"

Frank smiled. He sensed what was going through Jimmy's mind. "Bud can go with me tomorrow," Frank said. "It might be good for you, Jimmy, to know something about how to use a parachute properly."

"See you tomorrow, then," Jenny said. "I'll be waiting for you early!"

jimmy takes a parachute lesson

Jimmy awoke with a start. He hadn't slept well. Every time he fell off to sleep, his dreams went back to the sickening plunge he'd experienced in the Sierra Wave. Only, in his dream, the plane kept right on falling —down, down, down, into a deep, black abyss. It was a bottomless pit. The plane's wings broke off. He jumped out, but he'd forgotten his parachute!

To make matters worse, he'd listened to a news flash just before bedtime. The missing plane had been found by an Air Force helicopter pilot. There were no survivors.

The morning sun was just rising as Jimmy slowly got out of bed. He climbed into his clothes. He dreaded the coming day. He remembered Jenny's dare—and that he'd promised to make a jump with her. And nightmares had made things worse. He knew he couldn't go through with his promise.

Outside, Jimmy found Bud Horner, the young chief pilot, already at work in the big hangar. "What got you up so early?" Bud asked him. "It's barely six o'clock."

"Oh, I guess I didn't sleep much last night," Jimmy said. "I was thinking about a lot of things."

Bud put down his wrench. He motioned to Jimmy to sit down on an up-ended oil drum. "Let's talk about it," he said.

"Well," Jimmy began, "were you scared when you made your first parachute jump?"

Bud laughed. "So that's it! You've let Jenny get under your skin!"

Jimmy reddened. "She's only a girl! What does she know about flying?"

"Not as much as you do, Jimmy," Bud answered. "But she works pretty hard, doing what she likes best, the same as you."

"Oh, sure!" Jimmy said. "She just falls

₵O. SCHOOLS
C872342

out of an airplane. The parachute does all the work!''

''You know there's a lot more to jumping than that,'' Bud said. ''Remember the Army's crack jump team, the Golden Knights? You've really got to be sharp to join an outfit like that!''

Jimmy was silent. He'd seen the Golden Knights at air shows. The Knights were the world's top jumpers. But the thought of doing what they did was terrifying–making long, delayed jumps, trailing colored smoke, before pulling the ripcord. He couldn't tell even Bud about his fear of falling.

Bud sensed that something was wrong. He put his arm around Jimmy's shoulders. ''Sure. Jimmy, I was real scared on my first jump. But the fear went away the moment that big white canopy opened over my head.''

''Thanks, Bud,'' Jimmy said, forcing a smile. ''I'm going for a walk.'' He got up and went outside. He headed out across the desert. He tried to tell himself there was no reason to be afraid. Flying his sailplane, everything was fine. But flying a powered plane through the bucking, wrenching turbulence of the Sierra Wave was too much. He thought about the plane that had crashed out there, hammered to pieces because the pilot had lost control . . .

Maybe that's it, Jimmy mused. So long as you're in control, everything is fine. But if you go one step beyond–

A tiny cheep drew Jimmy's attention to an upper branch of a joshua tree. There was Sam, his pet falcon. He'd found Sam as a tiny fledgling, one day when the little fellow had fallen out of his nest. He had rescued the bird from the night animals that prowled the desert. He had taken the tiny creature home, and they had become fast friends. Once Sam had saved Jimmy's life, helping him find a thermal updraft when his sailplane was about to crash.

Now, Sam stretched his wings, made a short leap, and glided down over Jimmy's

head. He watched Sam swoop around in graceful climbing turns, searching for a morning thermal with his wingtip feathers. Finally he rose on silent wings and in seconds was barely a speck against the sky.

"Have a good flight, Sam!" Jimmy called. Then he suddenly checked his watch. It was after seven o'clock. He'd promised to meet Jenny early! Now she'd think he had deliberately stayed away–that he'd chickened out.

He broke into a trot. After all, he *couldn't* let Jenny think he was afraid. Maybe there was still time, if Bud would fly him over to Wilson Gorman's airport ten miles away. He found Bud outside the hangar, tuning up the engine of his little red sport biplane.

"Bud, can you fly me over to Gorman's?" Jimmy yelled over the noise of the engine.

"Sure!" Bud grinned. "But grab a chute–I want to practice some snaprolls on the way over."

Soon they were climbing into the morning sky, Jimmy strapped in the front seat, Bud

behind him. The little biplane suddenly
pitched up and the world seemed to spin
around and around. Then the plane's
wings came perfectly level. Jimmy loved
acrobatic flying. The way **Bud** did it, with
perfect timing and precision. There was
never anything unplanned, unexpected.

Jenny was waiting on the parking ramp when they taxied up in front of Gorman's big hangar. "You're late," she said. "I thought you'd be here early. I'd about decided you weren't coming."

"Bud and I were practicing his air show routine." Jimmy felt embarrassed.

"Well, come on," Jenny said impatiently. "I haven't got all day."

Silently, Jimmy followed her to the rear of the hangar where a parachute canopy was stretched out on a long, narrow rigging table. Jenny sat down on the table.

"Let's get something straight," she said. "Most everybody is afraid of jumping at first. But once you're floating down the sky, all alone between sky and earth, it's almost like being a bird."

Then Jenny went over every detail. How a parachute is made, what all its parts are for. What happens when you pull the ripcord and the little pilot chute pops out, dragging the big canopy behind it. She explained that sport jumpers wear two chutes—a back pack and a chest pack—just in case one fails to open.

"There used to be a joke jumpers told," Jenny said. "If the chute doesn't open, bring it back and get a new one. But with two chutes you needn't worry."

Jimmy nodded. He remembered Bud telling him, "When you know how things work, flying's safe. It's what you don't know that can hurt you." He had to admit that Jenny knew more than he did about parachutes. But still, there was much more to airmanship than jumping.

"Jenny," he said, after a while. "There's a CAP class tonight, at our hangar. You can learn lots of things that might surprise you!"

"Oh? Like what?" Jenny asked.

"Like what it takes to be a good pilot. All about airplanes and engines and radios—the weather and like that."

"How about parachute jumping?" Jenny asked, raising her eyebrows.

Jimmy shook his head. "No, not

parachute jumping. They won't let CAP Cadets jump. That's just a sport."

"And that's where you're dead wrong, Jimmy!" Jenny sounded annoyed. "What about paramedics, and smoke jumpers who fight forest fires, and–"

"Oh, all right," Jimmy said. "Maybe there's a place for it. Now, what else were you going to show me?"

"Come on out back–if you really want to learn something that can save your life some-day," Jenny said sharply.

Jimmy followed, keeping his ruffled feelings to himself. Jenny thought she knew everything! He watched her closely as she led the way around to the rear of the hangar. Any-how, she *was* sort of pretty–

"Here we are," Jenny said at last. "This is where you learn how to land without breaking a leg. They say it's not the fall that hurts you. It's the landing."

There was a deep sawdust pit below a platform ten feet above the ground. Jenny climbed up. "Watch," she said. "I'll show you what they call a parachute landing fall."

She relaxed her whole body, feet together, knees bent. She jumped and landed easily, and rolled over on her shoulder, her feet flying through the air. She stood up and dusted herself off.

"You don't break any bones that way," she said. "If there's a wind blowing, it can drag you over sharp rocks. Don't fight it. Roll with it."

"Is that how you twisted your ankle, up on Wild Horse Mesa?" Jimmy asked quickly. Then he wished he hadn't said it. Jenny was really trying to help.

"As a matter of fact, I hit a boulder," she answered. "I rolled over nice and easy, but the wind was too strong. It dragged me across a boulder field."

"I'm sorry," Jimmy said, meaning it. "Now, can I try a landing fall?"

Jenny nodded. Jimmy climbed the steps

to the platform. "Okay, watch!" he yelled. He hesitated and, for a moment, tried to imagine himself at the open door of a jump plane. He felt dizzy. He shut his eyes against the fear he suddenly felt.

"Eyes open," Jenny said softly, a half smile lurking at the corner of her mouth.

Jimmy sprang forward, forgetting to hold his feet together. Instead of rolling over, he fell flat on his face. He sat up, spitting sawdust.

Jenny laughed. "That's not the way I told you! Come on, try it again!"

Jimmy felt both embarrassed and annoyed. He was a good athlete. He could run a mile without getting winded. He had grown fast in the last year. He was tall and slender, taller than Jenny. Whatever the problem, he wouldn't quit. He sat up, brushed himself off, and tried again.

Soon he found he was making good progress with his parachute landing falls. Jenny finally led him back inside the hangar where an opened parachute hung from the rafters. She buckled Jimmy into the harness so that his feet were clear of the floor.

"Reach up and hold the risers," she told him. "If the wind blows you to one side, pull down with one hand, to spill air from the canopy. You'll slip back upwind that way.

Jimmy practiced. At last Jenny said, "Well, we've covered about everything– except how to leave the aircraft, and how to stabilize your body in free fall before the chute opens. How about tomorrow morning?"

"Oh, sure, I'll be here." But Jimmy's voice sounded a little weak.

Outside they heard the sound of an airplane landing. Bud had returned. Jimmy hurried to the plane, then turned to grin at Jenny.

"Thanks for the lesson on how to kill myself," he laughed. "See you tonight!"

jenny meets the civil air patrol

At 7 o'clock sharp Jenny Gorman took her scat in the front row, inside the Morning Sun Airfield hangar. Bud Horner was up front near a big blackboard, waiting for everybody to get settled. There were two dozen teen-agers, both boys and girls, in the group. Most of them wore the Civil Air Patrol uniform called fatigues.

Jimmy Fox dropped into the seat next to Jenny. "Bud's running the briefing tonight," he told her. "There'll be a CAP orientation talk. Then we'll study Search and Rescue."

Bud signaled for quiet. "Welcome aboard," he said. "I see several new faces tonight. So, first, I'll tell you a little about the Civil Air Patrol."

Bud smiled at Jenny as he talked about

CAP's emergency services: what CAP members do when an aircraft is missing; how the CAP goes into action during hurricanes, floods, forest fires and other disasters.

Jenny raised her hand. "Bud, how big is the Civil Air Patrol?" she asked.

"We have more than 2,000 units, divided into eight regions in this country," Bud answered. "Each region covers from five to nine states. There are fifty-two CAP Wings."

He explained that National CAP Headquarters was located at Maxwell Field, Alabama and that the CAP was an official civilian auxiliary of the United States Air Force. The CAP was born on December 1, 1941, he told his audience. For eighteen months, during World War II, CAP pilots flew offshore patrols, hunting German U-boats. They had spotted 173 and had sunk two, he said.

Bud described other CAP activities, then got down to the CAP Cadet program. He told Jenny and the other new visitors that the program was open to both boys and girls between the ages of thirteen and seventeen.

"What do we do in this program?" a boy asked from the back row.

"Well," Bud answered, "there's travel, adventure, aerospace study, to begin with. There's a week-long summer camp-out, usually at an Air Force base, and study courses in flight orientation and communications."

Jenny's eyes lighted up when Bud told about the International Cadet Exchange. "If you qualify," he told them, "you can go to any of twenty-two different countries for study. And there's the Cadet Solo Scholarship Program, for both boys and girls."

Jimmy nudged Jenny with his elbow. He whispered, "This is the best part!"

Bud went on to describe how cadets could compete for flight training by scoring high in studies, qualifying for fifteen hours of flight time, including two hours of solo flying. "You can even go to the Air Force Survival

School," Bud said. "You get special training in water survival, living off the land, and you learn how to live in the mountains without prepared food."

Bud glanced at his watch. "Let's take a five-minute break, then we'll go into search and rescue."

Jenny got up and went to Bud at the blackboard. "Bud," she asked, "doesn't the CAP have any parachute jumping courses?"

Bud grinned, then shook his head. "We don't allow CAP Cadets to jump, for safety reasons. If we need somebody to jump into a wreck site, we call in the pros–the Air Force paramedics."

He picked up a piece of chalk and turned to the blackboard. "Let's suppose a plane is down here, in a mountain meadow." He drew an X to mark the crash site. Then he drew another X, marking the spot where CAP rescue headquarters would be based, as near the wreck site as possible.

"This plane was seen to vanish from a

radar scope right about here," he said, pointing to a spot near the first X. "Another pilot picked up an ELT signal. He called the nearest Flight Service Station and they called in the Civil Air Patrol searchers."

Bud told Jenny how search planes carry automatic direction finders that point directly toward the ELT signal. "That way, they can fly directly to the wreck site," he explained.

Jenny was starting to ask another question, when the telephone on the hangar wall suddenly rang. Bud picked up the receiver. He spoke quickly, wrote something down, then hung up. He turned to the group, his face grim. "We've got a real emergency," he said quietly. "A plane is down in Sector X-Ray Twelve. Any volunteers?"

Jimmy jumped to his feet. "I'll go! And can Jenny go with me? It would be good practice for her!"

"Okay," Bud said shortly. "But let's hurry. Class dismissed!"

Soon they were flying north in the Cessna

180. Bud was in the pilot's seat, Jimmy beside him. Jenny rode in back. The night was black, except where a rising full moon peeked over the horizon to the east. It threw soft shadows across the desert and the mountains ahead.

Jimmy clamped on his headset. He tuned the radio to the emergency frequency—121.5 mHz. He heard a faint signal that sounded like *WOW! WOW! WOW!*

"Dead ahead, Bud!" Jimmy shouted.

Jenny grabbed a pair of binoculars. She began scanning the dark terrain below. There was little she could see—only vague shadows of joshua trees and rocky ridges.

Bud climbed the plane higher. At 10,000 feet they topped a ridge. Wild country stretched below. Death Valley lay beyond the Panamint Range to the east. Saline Valley lay ahead, a deep, isolated wilderness region. Jimmy heard the emergency signal growing louder. Jenny trained her binoculars on the valley ahead. "Over there," she cried, pointing to the right. "I see something!"

Jimmy could see a faint light, blinking on and off. Three short blinks...three long blinks...three short blinks...over and over. Someone with a flashlight was sending the international SOS distress signal.

Bud pushed the plane's nose down and dove toward the light in a high-speed power glide. Soon they could make out a small dirt landing strip in the moonlight. There was a wrecked plane at the far end where the light came from.

"Can we land here, in the dark?" Jimmy asked.

"We'll have to try," Bud answered. He circled low for a close look. He shook his head. "Looks bad," he said.

But they couldn't leave now. If they did, someone down there might die. Bud swung the plane around, lowered flaps, and turned on the landing lights.

Jimmy set his jaw. He saw that the runway was uneven, criss-crossed with gullies. Bud held off the landing until they passed the first deep gully, then chopped off power. The plane's wheels struck a rock. They bounced hard, veered off the runway, and spun around in a ground loop. "There goes the left tire!" Bud groaned. "Now we can't take off."

They all jumped out, Jimmy first, with Jenny and Bud close behind. They ran to the plane wreck, then stopped. The plane was a small two-seater, flipped over on its back. The pilot was pinned underneath. He was still waving his flashlight. Jenny knelt beside the injured man. "Are you hurt bad?" she asked.

The man's face was covered with blood from a bad cut on his forehead. He was shaking all over. "Sure thought I was done for!" he groaned. "I can't get free—my foot's stuck."

"Lend a hand, Jimmy," Bud ordered. Together they lifted the tail section of the wrecked plane, but not enough to free its pilot. Jenny called to them, "He's fainted! He must have lost a lot of blood!"

They lowered the plane's tail carefully, then tried to help Jenny pull the man free. Finally Jenny crawled into the crushed cockpit. She managed to pry the man's foot loose. They lifted him gently and carried him away from the wreckage.

The pilot regained consciousness. He tried to sit up. "Name's Elmer–Elmer Johnson," he said faintly. "My engine quit on me, flying over to Las Vegas. Hope you didn't hurt yourselves in that landing!"

Bud shook his head. "No, we just blew a tire. But now we can't fly you out! Jenny," he said, turning to the girl, "run and get the first aid kit. And Jimmy, put out a call on both CAP radio frequencies–147.8 and 143.7. Tell them what's happened!"

Jimmy ran to the Cessna 180 with Jenny. While she hurried back to Bud with the first aid kit, he turned on the radio, called the CAP. But there was no reply. The mountains surrounding the small valley had cut off all signals. Then he remembered that Bud had shut off the ELT. That meant the emergency channel, 121.5, was clear.

"Mayday! Mayday!" Jimmy called into the mike, on 121.5. "We've got an emergency! Does anybody hear me?"

Soon Jimmy made contact with an airline pilot, flying high overhead in the night sky. "This is Desert Airlines Flight 26," the voice said. "Go ahead."

Jimmy told the pilot what had happened. He asked him to call the CAP and relay his message. "Roger. Understand you need emergency airlift of injured pilot from Saline Valley," the voice stated. "We'll get them moving right away!"

The moon was high overhead when they heard the *chop-chop-chop* of a rescue helicopter in the distance. Soon it was over the tiny airstrip, shining bright spotlights down on them. In a few moments they had the injured pilot on board.

"We'll wait here," Bud told the rescuers. "And please have Frank Fox fly out with a new tire!"

Jimmy, Jenny and Bud watched the big chopper as it lifted off the runway, blowing a cloud of dust over them. Then it flew off into the night.

"We can't win 'em all, Jimmy," Bud

sighed.

"No, but we saved Elmer's life–and that's what counts," Jimmy said softly.

They sat quietly for awhile, watching the bright desert stars overhead. It would be six hours before daylight. Jenny's hand reached out and touched Jimmy's face. "I guess there are some things you can't do with a parachute," she said, her voice low. "And, Jimmy, thanks for bringing me along!"

jimmy makes the big leap

The telephone rang early one morning, a week after the rescue at Saline Valley. Jimmy jumped out of bed and hurried downstairs. He picked up the phone. It was Jenny. "Hi, Jimmy!" she said. "Did I wake you up?"

"It's only six o'clock," Jimmy answered sleepily. "What's up?"

"It's such a lovely morning," Jenny exclaimed. "I think this would be a great day for your first jump. Don't you?"

Jimmy gripped the receiver hard. He was too sleepy to think of a good excuse. "Well— I guess so, Jenny," he mumbled.

"That's great, Jimmy!" Jenny's voice was enthusiastic. "And can Bud fly the Cessna 180 for a jump ship? Dad's Bobcat is in the shop for engine work."

Jimmy was wide awake now. He was mad at himself. But it was too late to back out. He could have told Jenny he'd be busy flying the sailplane, or something. Instead, he heard himself saying, "Okay, I'll ask Bud. We'll be over in about an hour."

"That's fine, Jimmy!" Jenny said. "There's one more thing, a message from Dad. There's a charter flight scheduled for this morning, up to Reno, but Dad can't make it because the Bobcat is out of service. Can your father take the trip?"

Oh, this is going to be some day, Jimmy thought. "Well, I'll tell him." he answered. He hung up, feeling angry.

At breakfast Jimmy told Bud and his father what Jenny had said. Bud nodded. "I'll have to finish a periodic inspection of the Twin Beech D-18 to make that charter flight. Maybe Frances can fly the Cessna 180 for your jump."

"That's fine," Frances cut in. "I'll fly Jimmy over to Gorman's. Mom can handle the radio work here. Maybe Bud would like to make the trip with Dad, after he's finished the inspection?''

Bud nodded, his mouth full.

''You never know what the day will bring in this business,'' Frank Fox grinned. ''Good thing Jenny called early. Gives us time to get organized. And Jimmy–'' He set down his coffee cup. ''You listen carefully to what Jenny says. This'll be your first jump, won't it?''

''Yeah,'' Jimmy replied glumly. ''And maybe my last.''

Bud laughed. But his mother scolded him. ''That's not a funny joke, Jimmy. Now make your mind up. Either you go into this thing right, in a good frame of mind, or forget it.''

''All right!'' Jimmy half shouted. He pushed away from the table. He got up and started outside, but his father stopped him. ''Your mother's right, son,'' he said. ''Never go into the sky feeling angry about something. That way, you might do things wrong.

There's no room for mistakes in the sky."

"I'm sorry, Dad," Jimmy said. "I was just upset."

Frank Fox shoved Jimmy playfully, toward the door. "Now go make a fine jump. I want to hear a good report when I get back from the trip!"

Jimmy grinned back. He knew his father was right. He knew he'd try to do his best, in spite of the sickening fear he felt in his stomach. "Have a good trip, Dad," he said. "I'll do my best."

Bud followed Jimmy outside. "I'll take off the door of the 180. You'll need it off for your jump."

In the hangar Jimmy buckled the parachute harness over his CAP fatiques. The harness was the one he always wore when he flew aerobatics with Bud. Then he pulled on his jump boots and crash helmet. He swung his back pack chute over his shoulder, carrying it by the leg straps. A chest pack was already in the airplane.

Frances joined him. She looked over the 180 carefully, in a thorough preflight check. Then she slid into the left seat beside Jimmy and started the engine. Soon they were taking off, climbing into the morning sky. Jimmy tried not to think about the jump. There was no turning back now.

Jenny was waiting for them when they taxied up to the Gorman hangar. "This is your big day, Jimmy!" she said cheerfully. "You feel ready?"

"Oh, sure!" Jimmy forced a grin. "How high do we go?"

"Oh, about a mile will do fine," Jenny said. "Okay, Frances?"

"Climb aboard, Jenny," Frances answered. "We're all set."

Jimmy rode in back with Jenny as Frances climbed the plane eastward toward the drop zone Jenny had chosen. It was not far from Wild Horse Mesa, but there was no wind. To the north a curved lenticular cloud was just forming over the Sierras. Jimmy pointed.

"There's a lenny!" he shouted over the noise of the wind blowing past the open door. "Looks like Dad and Bud are in for some weather."

"Keep your mind on what you're doing, Jimmy," Jenny shouted back. "You go out first, then I'll follow. Remember, keep your feet on the wheel. Frances will lock the brakes. Grab hold of the wing strut and hang on until I signal you to push back."

Jimmy glanced outside the open door, then down. He could hardly breathe. He felt dizzy. looking at the ground thousands of feet below. He wanted to call the whole thing off. But there was no way. Frances slowed the plane, then headed into the west. Jenny slapped Jimmy on the back. "On your way, cowboy!"

Jimmy breathed deep. "Okay, ugly," he grinned.

Jenny punched at him playfully as he groped his way through the door, into the tearing slipstream. He stepped down onto the

wheel, the way he'd practiced on the ground under Jenny's guidance.

He stared straight ahead, fearful of looking down at the ground so far below. His fingers found the wing strut and closed around it. He wondered if he could actually let go. His old fear of falling swept over him, making him feel giddy. He wanted to scream into the wind, *"No, I can't do it!"*

He clung to the wing strut for dear life. Desperately, he wanted to climb back inside the cabin. But Jenny was leaning out the open doorway. *"Go!"* she yelled into the wind.

For a second Jimmy clung there, frozen with fear. Then, almost without thinking, he shoved hard and flung his arms wide. He spread his legs at the same time in order to stay stable. The plane pulled away. Then he was falling, falling, down the sky.

Now he remembered to cross his arms over his chest, the fingers of his right hand groping for the ripcord handle. Where was

it? He found it–and pulled hard, remembering not to let it go. The pilot chute popped out behind him, dragging the main canopy out into the vertical wind. There was a sudden jerk. He was yanked upright. He looked up. The parachute canopy formed a huge white cloud overhead.

All fear left him. He felt suddenly free! He was really a part of the sky now. Floating on the wind, like a soaring bird—

The sound of the airplane faded in the distance. Jimmy saw Jenny's body plunging down the sky, her arms folded back so that she seemed to be falling faster than an arrow. Suddenly her chute blossomed out. She floated alongside Jimmy, only a short distance away.

"You did great, Jimmy!" she yelled over to him. "Now, spill some air and slip toward the north."

Jimmy reached up and pulled down on the risers on one side. He felt himself slipping to that side. Then he let go and was again floating straight down.

Jenny shouted encouragement as he drifted toward the open space she'd picked for their drop zone. It was next to a small dirt landing strip. Jimmy forgot to be afraid. It was all so—new, and it was beautiful. A whole new world was opening up to him. He

would never be afraid of falling again. The parachute harness held him securely in its grip.

"Prepare to land!" Jenny's voice cried. Jimmy held his feet together. He bent his knees slightly, folding his arms over his chest pack to protect his face. The ground rushed up at him. Then his feet hit the ground. He rolled forward smoothly, over one shoulder. When he came to a stop he got to his feet and spilled the air from the canopy by pulling on the risers.

Then Jenny came running toward him. Before he knew what was happening, she had thrown her arms around him and was kissing him hard. Jimmy blushed and wiped his mouth on his forearm. Then they both laughed. Jimmy wanted to tell her how he felt—a wonderful, warm glow inside of him.

"Well, I did it," was all he could think of to say.

"No, Jimmy," Jenny said softly. "This is just the beginning!"

The Cessna 180 landed on the dirt strip. Jimmy and Jenny walked over to it, carrying their chutes. They climbed in. "Congratulations, Jimmy!" Frances said. Then she swung the ship's tail around, gunned the engine, and they took off for home.

the

mountain

rescue

Jimmy and Jenny, riding in the back seat, looked out through the open doorway as Frances Fox piloted the Cessna toward Morning Sun Airfield. It had been an exciting morning. Jimmy felt very proud. He felt as though a great weight had been lifted. He had conquered his fear of falling—at last.

Suddenly the radio in the cockpit came to life. "Frances," a voice said, "this is Mother! Come in, Frances!" Jimmy was startled. His mother was not using the CAP code.

Quickly Frances Fox picked up the mike. "This is Frances. Mother, what is it?"

"Hurry back—as fast as you can!" Debbie Fox's voice was shaking. "Dad and Bud are in trouble."

Jimmy's stomach tightened into a knot.

What could be the matter? Then he remembered the lenticular cloud! The Sierra Wave was blowing–and it was right in their path.

Debbie Fox was waiting for them when they landed. "They got caught in a storm!" she said, her face white. "Dad radioed that their wings had iced up. The plane was forced down – somewhere up there in those awful mountains!"

Frances turned to Jimmy and Jenny. She spoke calmly. "Get your emergency gear. And fresh chutes."

Jimmy and Jenny ran to the hangar. They gathered up a supply of survival gear and two newly packed parachutes. Debbie Fox met them back at the plane, a thermos of hot coffee and sandwiches in her hands.

"Stay on the air," she said to Frances. "I'll call you if I hear anything from the CAP Wing Headquarters. Be sure to call me *immediately* when you get a fix on them!"

Frances swung the plane around and in a moment they were off the ground. They had enough fuel for four hours of flying. But it would be terribly cold with the plane's right door off. There had been no time to put it back on.

The plane climbed higher and higher. At 14,000 feet they crossed the highest peaks of the snow-capped Sierras. Here they began their search of the icy meadows below. Up ahead, the lenticular cloud hung across the sky like some evil omen. The highest of the mountain peaks were shrouded in black storm clouds. Snow flurries whipped against the plane. They stuck to the windshield so that the searchers had to look out the open door in order to see.

A fierce downdraft slammed the plane with brutal force, tipping it into a near-vertical bank. Jimmy caught his breath, waiting to feel the awful fear which had numbed him before. But the fear did not come.

A slow grin curved Jimmy's lips. He was in complete control of himself now. The fear was gone! He leaned forward quickly and

picked up the mike. "White Bear Ten-Ten," he called. "This is Brown Bear Ten-Eight. Come in, Ten-Ten!"

"Go ahead, Brown Bear Ten-Eight." His mother's voice sounded steadier.

"We're over the Bishop Cups now," he told her. "Storm is getting worse up here. No joy on the Twin Beech!"

Jimmy was instinctively using the military CAP jargon. *No joy* meant *no contact*. The search was still in progress. He tuned the radio to 121.5, the emergency frequency. Suddenly the radio went *WOW! WOW! WOW!* An ELT must have gone off!

"ELT contact." Jimmy shouted. "We've got them!"

Swiftly his fingers tuned the automatic direction finder to 121.5. The ADF needle swung around, pointing directly toward a high mountain peak at their left.

"Over there!" Jimmy yelled to his sister. "They're down somewhere over there– in that valley!"

Jimmy switched radio channels once more, this time to 143.7, the CAP emergency frequency. "This is Brown-Bear Ten-Eight!" he called. "Dad, can you hear me?"

There was a burst of static as a lightning bolt stabbed the sky close by. Then a voice said, "Brown Bear Ten-Eight, this is Bud. We can hear your engine overhead–but we can't see you! It's snowing too hard."

"Is Dad–all right?" Jimmy called.

"A broken leg, Jimmy," Bud answered. "Got to get out of here by tonight or we'll both freeze!"

Jimmy acted smoothly, efficiently. His mind was calm, his actions direct. He called home base and reported in. Then he turned to Jenny. "Chute up," he yelled. "We're jumping in!"

Jimmy went out first. He stepped out into the freezing wind. In a moment he was falling free, through a white curtain of blowing snow. He pulled the ripcord. The chute opened and he jerked to a stop. He saw

Jenny's chute blossom close by. "Head for the middle of the valley!" he shouted to her.

Jimmy could barely see the Beech D-18 down below. A wing was broken off. Then the blowing snow closed over the downed plane and he could see nothing at all. He held his feet together, knees bent, then waited. Seconds later he struck the ground, quickly rolling over into a snowbank. He unbuckled his chute, grabbed his emergency kit, then struggled through the deep snow toward the plane wreck.

He heard Jenny's voice calling to him. He looked up, startled. She was hanging by her chute's riser cords from the branches of a tall pine tree. "Unbuckle your harness!" he yelled. "I'll catch you when you drop!" Jenny struggled free, then let go. She dropped ten feet, feet first, into Jimmy's arms. He swung her to the ground.

Together they hurried to the plane wreck. Bud was sitting on the broken wing, holding his head. His head was covered with blood.

"Frank's still in the cockpit," he said. Jimmy crawled inside the cabin. He groped his way to the cockpit, while Jenny gave Bud first aid.

Jimmy found his father slumped in the left seat of the plane. Frank Fox looked up at him. He smiled weakly. "Shouldn't have risked your neck, son," he said.

"Let's get you out of here, Dad," Jimmy answered. "Can you move?"

"A little. But it sure hurts!"

Jimmy dragged his father through the door of the plane. With Jenny's help he lifted him onto its wing. Frank Fox groaned. "We tried to turn back," he murmured. "Too much ice on the wings . . ."

"Mom has alerted Wing Headquarters," Jimmy told him confidently. "But we're going to get you out *now*. You both need help fast!"

Bud had slipped into unconsciousness from loss of blood. Jenny was wiping his face with a rag. "Keep an eye on Dad too," Jimmy said to her. He hurried off to the nearest tree and broke off several of its branches. Then he went to the plane's left engine which had been torn off the wing. The engine cowling lay split open.

Jimmy dragged the metal cowling out from under the wreckage. He bent it into the shape of a crude toboggan, then stacked the branches on top. With Jenny's help, he laid the two injured men on the rough bed.

He moved swiftly and efficiently. He found a piece of canvas in the wreckage and spread it over Bud and his father. It would help in protecting them from the icy wind.

He turned to Jenny. He had tied a rope to the front end of the sled. "Lend a hand," he said. "We've *got* to get Dad and Bud off the mountain fast! Down into Owens Valley, where it's warmer."

"Shouldn't we stay by the wreck so that the rescue planes can find us?" Jenny asked.

Jimmy shook his head firmly. "Nobody can find us in this storm. Fran has flown home by now and it'll be hours before anybody else can fly in!"

Suddenly he remembered something. He

ran to the wreckage to find the ELT. He removed it from its bracket and carried it to the sled. That done, he and Jenny began the long, hard trek through the snowfield. They headed toward the east, dragging the sled with the two unconscious men behind them. After an hour they stopped for breath. Jimmy pulled a chart from the emergency kit.

While he studied the map, Jenny tried to make the injured men comfortable. They seemed barely to be breathing. She tucked the canvas cover more tightly about them to preserve their body heat.

Jimmy put away the chart. "Just a few more miles." he said to Jenny. "Then we should pick up the down trail into Owens Valley, over into the John Muir Wilderness Area–right over there." He pointed toward the east. "I've camped up here and know the country pretty well."

It seemed as though hours had passed before they finally dragged the sled into a clearing. It lay at the top of a steep wall of

granite rearing itself high above the valley. The two men seemed to be awake. Jenny poured hot coffee from the thermos and gave each of them a sip.

"Jimmy," she whispered very softly. "Your father and Bud need medical attention *fast!* They'll die if we don't get help soon! What shall we do?" Jimmy saw tears in her eyes.

Jimmy Fox didn't answer. He was thinking hard. It seemed to him that he had grown up fast—in the last few hours. He had risked his life and Jenny's to save his father and Bud. He was no longer a boy hiding a secret fear. He was making hard decisions, acting on them surely, like an adult.

"We've got two choices, Jenny," he told her at last. "We can stay here and build a fire. The snow should clear up soon. Or we can try to make it down the trail. Of course that's pretty dangerous, dragging the sled."

Jenny hesitated. Then she said, "It's up to you, Jimmy. You'll have to decide."

A patch of light suddenly showed overhead. The clouds were thinning! Blue sky showed, then was instantly covered up again by the swirling clouds. All at once they heard a voice on the mobile radio fastened to Jimmy's belt.

"Black Bear Ten-Fourteen! Come in, Black Bear! Do you copy?"

Jimmy grabbed the mobile unit. "This is Black Bear Ten-Fourteen!" he cried into the mike.

"Roger, Black Bear!" came the reply. "This is Air Force Rescue Helicopter Blue Goose. We're just north of Mt. Whitney. What is your position?"

Jimmy glanced at his chart, then reported, "We're right at the top of Piute Pass!"

The *throb-throb-throb* of a helicopter soon sounded somewhere overhead, echoing from the surrounding rocks. Jimmy and Jenny watched the chopper breaking through the clouds, settling slowly into the clearing. It hovered close to the snow pack. Three paramedics jumped out.

They hurried quickly to examine the injured men. Then they lifted them carefully onto wire litters and carried them to the waiting helicopter. "Okay, you're next!" one of them called to Jimmy and Jenny.

When the chopper was aloft Jimmy leaned back against the side of the big cabin and closed his eyes. He felt suddenly tired. The helicopter swung out over the valley, away from the rocky cliffs, and made its way carefully down Piute Pass. Soon they came to Bishop Airport where they landed. An ambulance was waiting for them.

A nurse took over, to give the injured men injections. Soon they were awake. Frank Fox sat up. "You did a good job, son," he said. "Both you and Jenny."

Bud looked at Jenny who was bending over him. "You still want to join the Civil Air Patrol?" he asked her.

"You bet!" Jenny answered, then laughed.

Jimmy cut in. "I just hope the CAP won't be mad at us for jumping in–against the rules. We did it on our own, of course."

"I think they won't be mad, Jimmy," Bud said. "Not the way things turned out!"

Jimmy Fox stared through the window of the Cessna 180 at the jagged snow-capped peaks of the Sierra Nevada Mountains directly below him. There was no sign of the missing plane. A few hours before, Jimmy and his father, Frank Fox, had taken off from Morning Sun Airfield on the Mojave Desert on a Civil Air Patrol Search and Rescue mission in response to an emergency call. At fifteen, Jimmy was proud to be a Cadet in the nationwide CAP program, a civilian auxiliary of the United States Air Force. Though it would be another year before he could obtain a license to fly on his own, he was already an old hand as a CAP observer. Each mission was a challenge. Its success could spell the difference between life and death to a pilot in trouble. These new adventures of Jimmy, hero of *Jimmy Fox And The Flying Falcon* (published in 1977 by Childrens Press), make an even more exciting story than its predecessor, filled with suspense from beginning to end. The author has gathered his material concerning the Civil Air Patrol's far-flung activities from first-hand sources, thereby giving the book a welcome ring of complete authenticity and authority.

Don Dwiggins has written more than a dozen books, both fiction and non-fiction, about almost every aspect of flying. A seasoned airman, he truly speaks from experience, for he has flown all sorts and kinds of aircraft, from gliders and home-builts to today's most advanced powered planes. His flying career began in World War II as an instructor in Britain's Royal Air Force. Today he flies his own plane and has logged more than 10,000 flying hours as a first pilot. During a distinguished writing career, Mr. Dwiggins has contributed thousands of aviation articles to newspapers and national magazines and was aviation editor of two large metropolitan dailies. With his wife Olga, he spends vacations in the wilds of Canada where he built a summer cabin entirely by hand.

Olga Dwiggins was born in Ontario, Canada, and grew up in the Canadian North Woods. She says that she first learned to draw and paint during both winter and summer camp-outs with her young brothers where she attempted to capture on sketch pad and canvas the beauty of the landscape surrounding her. From this early beginning she determined to become a professional artist and came to the United States to take her formal art training. She attended the Otis Art Institute and Art Center, both in Los Angeles. Her marriage to Don Dwiggins has led her to many adventures in the out-of-doors, including a glider trip over California's Mojave Desert, the locale of the books about Jimmy Fox. The Dwiggins' fly cross-country each summer (accompanied by their three Yorkshire terriers) to their island retreat where they write and paint.